GRAVE
MATTER

Juno Dawson

GRAVE MATTER

With illustrations by
Alex T. Smith

Barrington Stoke

To Darren – as wise
as he is kind-hearted

First published in 2017 in Great Britain by
Barrington Stoke Ltd
18 Walker Street, Edinburgh, EH3 7LP

www.barringtonstoke.co.uk

Text © 2017 Juno Dawson
Illustrations © 2017 Alex T. Smith

The moral right of Juno Dawson and Alex T. Smith to be
identified as the author and illustrator of this work has been
asserted in accordance with the Copyright, Designs and
Patents Act, 1988

A CIP catalogue record for this book is available
from the British Library upon request

ISBN: 978-1-78112-604-2

Printed in China by Leo

"The boundaries which divide Life from Death are at best shadowy and vague. Who shall say where the one ends, and where the other begins?"

EDGAR ALLAN POE – *THE PREMATURE BURIAL*

1

There is still snow on the ground when they lower her into it. The same snow, I suppose, as the night she died.

I'm drunk. Everything is fuzzy at the edges. My eyelids are sore and swollen, my blinking sluggish. A vodka filter. The snowy graveyard swims in and out of focus. If I squint, grey stick-men cluster around her grave.

All is black and white, with only the lilacs atop her coffin for colour. They were her favourite.

Don't let me go.
    I won't.

She gripped my hand. Pale fingers, ebony nails.
Please, Samuel ...
I promise I won't. I won't let you go.
Her grip went slack.

My father is sombre, professional, as stiff as his vicar's collar. It is his job to be solemn, but I wonder if today he means it. I think he must – everyone who met Eliza loved her.

"In the Name of God," my father begins, "the merciful Father, we commit the body of our daughter and friend Eliza Grey to the peace of the grave."

Mrs Grey is wailing, burying her face in the lapel of Mr Grey's coat. Her pained cries – animal somehow – soar and swoop through the naked winter trees, shaking crows from the branches. Tears stream down her chin. No one knows what to do to comfort her. Other mourners politely ignore her grief. They shift from foot to foot, unsure of what to do with their hands.

My limbs feel too long and limp, like over-done spaghetti.

The coffin is lowered into the earth. At the flick of a switch, the device cranks and wheezes to life and the coffin descends. It seems too small by far to contain Eliza. It's all wrong. To box her is grotesque, like caging a hummingbird.

Are you OK to drive in this weather?

Of course, it's not that bad.

I don't know, Sam, that snow is pretty seriously snowy.

It'll be fine, it's not even settling. Promise. We'll be home in ten.

Every time I close my eyes I see that moment play on a loop. Eliza looked out of the bay window at Fish's house, watching feathery flakes swirl under the street lights. That was the fork in the road. We could have spent the night at Fish's.

But we didn't. We took the other prong. I made her.

Father stands where the headstone will be. He goes on and on.

"Earth to earth, ashes to ashes, dust to dust. May the Lord bless her and keep her, the Lord make his face to shine upon her and be gracious unto her, the Lord lift up his face upon her and give her everlasting peace. Amen."

Amen.

My father throws the first dirt on top of Eliza's coffin. We must all play our part in burying her. The mud rains down on the lilacs, spoiling them. Next, Mr Grey steps forward, Mrs Grey still under his arm. He too throws dirt over his daughter.

It's all too much. We can't ... we can't smother Eliza like this. How ... how will she breathe down there? She doesn't belong in the dark and cold. She was scared of the dark.

I fall to my knees. I feel icy slush seep into my

trousers. "No!" I cry, and I reach for Eliza's coffin far below. I scramble to the edge of the grave. "No, you can't! Eliza!"

Burly hands grab my arms and drag me away. I kick and struggle, but strangers hold me back. Mrs Grey wails anew. Father looks so disappointed.

Mother's hand unfurls and I see that a tiny, pale blue pill rests in her palm. "Here," she says. "Take this. You'll feel better."

Her lips are taut, her eyes stern. She – Dr Beauvoir – knows best.

"What is it?" I ask.

"Just take it, Samuel. You need to rest. You haven't slept since the crash. I hear you pacing around."

"I don't want it."

"Just. Take. It."

Reluctant – because I worry I'll be stuck in the nightmare – I swallow the pill. Mother grips my face to check under my tongue. "Good boy. Now, I'd better get over to the Wake."

"I should be there."

"After your performance at the graveyard? I don't think so. Sleep. We'll be back to check on you in a few hours, but your father needs to be there."

She helps me out of my black blazer and I pull off my tie. My curtains – thick crimson velvet like all the others in our house, the rectory – are shut. They block out every drop of crisp winter light. "Now, lie down."

I do as I'm told and she pulls the patchwork quilt up over me. "Mum ..."

"Yes?"

"I don't ... I don't know what to do without her ... I can't live without –"

"Samuel, don't even say it." Mum perches on the edge of my bed and her pine green eyes soften. The same eyes as mine. Eliza told me she loved my weird eyes. "I've seen this a million times," Mum goes on. "Don't tell your dad I took His name in vain, but oh God, the grief will hurt like hell but it won't last for long. I promise. Every day it'll get better as you forget –"

"I don't want to forget her!"

She strokes my hair. It's short, a number-two shave all over, and her touch comforts me. It reminds me of being a child. "That's not what I meant," Mother says. "You won't forget Eliza, you'll forget the pain. Eliza wouldn't want to see you like this and you know it."

I feel the sleeping pill start to take effect. My head feels like it's full of black water that's sloshing around my skull. I say nothing.

"Now sleep." Mother leans in and kisses my forehead. "Sweet dreams." She switches off the lamp and I don't even notice the darkness any more.

2

My dreams are colourful swill. I toss and turn as my brain tries to resist whatever drug Mother made me take. Shallow half-visions wash over my mind then ebb away.

Of all the memories that return to me, I don't know why I remember *that* visit to Mr Hargreaves' office. It was last autumn, the sun glowed through amber leaves and I wanted to be outside. I was hungry too, but first we had to deal with Callum Brookes.

Eliza was livid. "Oh *come on*," she said as she tucked a lock of chestnut hair behind her ear. "Mr Hargreaves, it's absurd. I mean 'meninist'? It's not even a word."

"Yes it is," Callum said. He leaned back in his chair, his legs spread as wide as his trousers would permit. I sat between him and Eliza, keeping them apart. "It's on the internet so it's a word."

Mr Hargreaves pinched the top of his nose. "Eliza, if you're allowed your Feminism Club, I don't see why Callum can't ..."

Eliza took a deep breath. "OK. Can Callum explain exactly which rights his club is trying to defend?"

Callum shrugged. "Like, the right to be a man."

"Ah yes," Eliza said. "You must feel so oppressed by all those male authors we read in English and all the male scientists, kings and explorers we learn about. It must be a real drag that you can't take part in *girls' sports* or wear a ra-ra skirt in P.E. while boys leer from the side of the netball court. And it's a shame you can't wear these pervy kilts that freeze your legs off in winter. In truth, Brother – your struggle is real."

"That's not what I'm saying." Callum squirmed in his seat.

"No," Eliza went on. She had him on the ropes now. "What you're saying is you want another way to assert yourself over the girls by taking away the one thing at this school that was about girls and girls only. You won't even let us have our bloody club, will you?"

"Well, it's not fair!" Callum protested.

"Yes it is," I added. "Boys are allowed to attend the Feminism Club. We encourage it, as a matter of fact. We don't need a separate club for men's rights."

"There aren't any rights you don't already have," Eliza finished.

The walls of Hargreaves' office crumble and fade at the edges. I'm no longer in an office chair. I'm in the driver's seat. I can't fight it. The heater in my clapped-out Astra blasts on my soggy trainers, making the car smell like burnt toast. The windscreen wipers bat away big moth-like snowflakes. Beside me, Eliza is wrapped in a woolly scarf and beanie hat. "It's really coming down now," she says. "I wonder if we'll get the day off tomorrow. Snow day!"

"A-woo-hoo! I hope so," I tell her. "I have that Biology test, so I fully support that."

"Look! People have abandoned their cars."

"Oh, it's not that bad," I say. "I'll drive down by the high street so we don't have to attempt Park Hill."

Through the blizzard, I see the junction coming up and I know what's about to happen. I can't. I can't do it again.

I force my brain to go somewhere else. I drag myself into a different dream.

The snowflakes turn into blossom.

I'm in the garden at home. There's the pond with its lily pads and reeds. The fountain babbles. A heron – Dad's arch-enemy – tries to pinch the fish even though there's a net over the pond now. Willow branches droop over the walls and a handsome apple tree stands in the middle of the lawn, from which the candy-pink blossom twirls.

I roll across the grass, laughing and laughing. I can't breathe I'm laughing so much. The lawn has just been mown and it smells of spring. The sun is high and pale, the sky periwinkle blue.

Aunt Marie lies alongside me. "Oh my days," she cackles. "I can't keep up with you, Samuel. I'm an old woman!"

"You're not old!" My voice sounds very young. I *am* very young. I don't remember this. Aunt Marie hasn't visited us in *years*. Dad wouldn't let her in the front door.

In the dream, she tickles me under my arms and I scream with joy. She's wearing a loose cotton dress, and a headscarf over her long braids. Bangles and beads clatter on her wrists. "Life lesson. Flattery gets you everywhere, young man!"

There's a sudden cry from the back of the garden, down by the rose bushes. "Oh, Socks, no! Get off it!"

I roll over and see Mum grab the cat, a big fat tabby. That cat has been dead for years now. "Poor thing."

She carries Socks up the garden path to the house. "What's he done, Mel?" Marie asks.

"He's got a little dicky bird. Oh, he's always bringing us presents. Nightmare. I'll put him inside."

"Is it dead?" I ask. I'm already running towards the rose bushes. Mum shouts an answer, but I don't hear her. A broken bird lies among the thorny, twisted rose bushes. I think it's a sparrow – brown with a black crest and beak. It's caked in blood, its wings wide. "Aw," I say.

The poor thing twitches, trying to right itself.

"It's alive," Aunt Marie says, as she appears at my side. I go to pick it up. "No, don't touch it, you might make it worse."

"But if we leave it there, Socks will come back out and finish it off."

Aunt Marie kneels down, hitching up her skirt. "Let me get a look at it. Step aside, Sam." Marie reaches out and cups her hands around the bird. It tweets and tweets, cries and cries. It would have been kinder if Socks had killed it. Oh so gently, Marie scoops the sparrow up.

With the bird safe in her palms, Aunt Marie closes her eyes and raises her hands to her plum lips. She whispers something through the gap where her thumbs meet. Her mouth moves, but I can't hear what she's saying. She starts to rock back and forth as she mutters to the bird. Her words don't sound like English.

"Aunt Marie?" I ask. I'm confused and a little scared.

She ignores me. Her eyes pop open and for a second they roll back into her head, totally white and wild. Then she opens her hands and the sparrow shoots out – up and up and away into the tree tops. When I look back to Aunt Marie, her eyes are normal again and she's smiling as she watches the bird vanish into the wide blue sky.

She looks down at me. "It's fine," she says with a broad grin. "It just needed picking up and dustin' off a little. He'll think twice before he comes to this garden again!"

"What did you do?" I ask, awestruck.

"I didn't do nothing," Aunt Marie says with a wink.

I awake with a jolt. My eyes are fuzzy and my head is like glue from the sleeping pill but, even in the dark, I see something move. Right above my face, a white spider hangs from a line of web. Its needle legs flex just inches from my eyes.

I'm not a fan of spiders.

I swear and roll away.

The spider – so pale it's almost see-through – scuttles up its web to the ceiling. I flick the lamp on and see that it's after midnight – I've been asleep for

hours. When I look back up, I
can't see the ghostly spider. It
must have scurried off into a nook.

I'm wide awake now. I turn the
lamp off and lie back down. But I
know I won't go back to sleep. I can't
even close my eyes.

I think about Eliza – laughing,
smiling, throwing her wet hair back in the
park. It was last July, and we were having
a water fight. I think about her trying to
cry silently during a sad movie so no one
would notice. Then I think about the time we
watched the sun set on Brighton beach. That
day was the most perfect day.

But then I think about the black Range Rover
that glided across the junction like an ice skater.
I think about how I swerved the car to avoid it.

I think about Aunt Marie.

I think about the sparrow.

3

With the funeral over, life is supposed to go on,
business as usual. I slip in and out of wafer-thin
sleep for the rest of the night, then feel disconnected
as I trudge downstairs, like my feet are a couple
of millimetres off the carpet. I grip the dark wood
banister for support. Everything in the rectory is
stern – the wood panels, the oppressive drapes, the
vases and trinkets. Sometimes I feel like I live in a
museum.

I hear Mother and Father in the kitchen. We have
a dining room, but it's for show, only used when we
have fancy guests, otherwise there's a more homely,
everyday table in the kitchen.

"Why aren't you in your uniform?" Mother asks. She's cradling an enormous mug of coffee and smoking the first of her three Marlboro Lights of the day.

"I can't go in today," I say, my throat tight. I'm in the clothes I grabbed from the top of the wash basket – jeans and a T-shirt.

Mrs Fanshaw, the housekeeper, tuts. "You'd do best to get back into a routine, Samuel. That's what I did after our Stan passed on." She carries a rack of toast to the table. A flowery apron stretches across her formidable bust.

"I do think Mrs F's right," Mother agrees. "You've got to get back into the swing of things as soon as possible. Normal, usual things will do you good."

Dad sets his coffee down. He's in his black shirt, but his white collar is undone for now. "Samuel, my boy, that's what the funeral is for ... it's a chance to say goodbye. Eliza is at rest now. Blessed are the dead who die in the Lord."

He reaches for my hand, but I pull it back with more anger than I intend. "I'm not one of your flock, Dad. I don't need a sermon. I need Eliza."

The kitchen goes very quiet. After all, we're English and we're not supposed to express our feelings. Mrs Fanshaw shuffles over to the sink. Dad's nostrils flare. "You know as well as I do that Eliza is in a better place," he tells me.

Hot red shapes – triangles and squares – flash in front of my eyes and curses fill my head. I want to scream in Dad's face that I don't believe that shit for a second. I don't think Eliza is a sunbeam. I think she's dead, and I think God is a bastard too or there's no way Eliza would be dead. I want to hit Dad, I want to punch his stupid righteous face, I want to beat the faith out of him the way he's bored it out of me.

I wish I were dead.

But I bite my tongue. "I'm not going back today."

They share a meaningful glance.

"Very well," Mother says as she stubs out her cigarette. "One more day. But you go back tomorrow. It's your last year and you can't miss something you might need in your exams."

"It's what Eliza would have wanted," Dad says.

"You don't know that. You didn't know her," I snap. A bitter taste fills my mouth. I push myself away from the table and leave the kitchen.

I sit in the bath until the house falls quiet. I lie under the water until my lungs feel like they'll explode then I surface, gasping for air. I'd do it, I'd let myself drown, but I don't believe Eliza will be waiting for me on the other side. I simply do not believe Father's stories. I wonder if the endless black nothing of death would be better or worse than being here without her.

Sure, I have friends, but they were *our* friends.

SamAndEliza. We've been together so long, everyone thinks of us as a single unit. Seeing them will only make me miss her more. I'll feel like half a thing.

I get out of the bath and make it as far as my bed. I rest there for a second. I'm tempted to pull the covers over my head and wait for night again, but the dream still rattles around my skull.

Aunt Marie. The sparrow. Its beating wings.

I get dressed properly – clean underwear and a winter jumper. Eliza liked this one – she always said she could see reindeer in the pattern. I told her she was imagining it, it was just a pattern.

I lean over the banister to check Mrs Fanshaw has finished for the morning. That old busybody. She's a walking library of parish gossip – the Sin Collector. Mother only agreed to give her a job because Father felt sorry for her after her husband died. "Mrs Fanshaw?" I call.

There's no reply so I hurry downstairs, barefoot. Father's study is never locked – because *we trust each other.* In fairness, I've never wanted to sneak in until today. I slip inside and close the door. It's mid-morning, but the room is murky and grey. I flick the light on.

Everything is neat and in order. A skin-and-bone Jesus hangs on a cross, pain carved into his wooden face. There are shelves and shelves of books about how to read The Book, which always seems odd to me. The sleek Mac looks out of place on the walnut desk, but modern priests have to keep modern records.

I don't even know what I'm looking for. An address book? I sit in Dad's big leather chair and work my way through the desk drawers. There is an organiser, but it's all work contacts – the bishop, plumbers, steeplejacks and so on.

I know, all the way to my bones, that I need to contact Aunt Marie right now. She and Dad had a huge argument when I was about eleven. I wasn't there and no one told me what it was about, but all of a sudden, Marie was no longer invited for Christmas and Easter. My questions about where she was were not well received.

At the bottom of the bottom drawer are some old-fashioned files and binders. I pull them out and hidden underneath is a bundle of letters held with a rubber band. Our address is written on the front and I know right away they're from Aunt Marie. There are five in total, and Father hasn't even opened the last two.

I daren't open those, but I look at the top letter. It's dated three years ago.

Dear Henri,

I hope you, Mel and Samuel are well. It seems we're as stubborn as each other, but don't you think this has gone on for too long now? You have your opinion and I have mine, but we are blood.

From the bottom of my heart I miss you and

I hope we can put aside our differences and talk again.

We believe in the same one God and I hope you can find it in your heart to forgive me.

Love always, all ways.
Marie.

The other two letters are much the same – Marie pleading with Father to get in touch. Most importantly, all five letters were sent from the same address in Brixton.

I've found her.

4

The train carriage is almost empty at this time of day. Its windows are steamed up, the seats covered in croissant crumbs, crumpled *Metro*s and lipstick-marked Starbucks coffee cups with their holders around their ankles. I sit alone, too tired to read or play on my phone. I stare at the city skyline.

It's six stops and fifty minutes into London Liverpool Street. There, I join the procession of zombies to the Underground. Everyone looks down. No one looks me in the eye.

I don't know London all that well. But at last I find my way to Brixton on the Victoria line. What did people do before Google Maps? Marie's flat is supposed to be a ten-minute walk from the station in the direction of Stockwell.

There's no snow in the city. Instead the pavements are covered in slick, slimy dirt and patches of black ice. Brixton is noisy and smelly, a market stall burns incense right outside the tube station. A homeless man with long grey dreadlocks limps at me, asking for change. At home, I always feel like I might as well be black. Right now, I feel very white.

I try hard not to wave my new phone around as I follow the Google Map. I leave the hustle and bustle behind and head for the quieter streets. Huge concrete blocks loom over me – and I realise Persephone House must be one of these. I soon find myself in a warren of ugly, pebble-dash cubes, the rusty fire escapes like braces on rotten teeth. The map sends me down alleys and shortcuts I wish it wouldn't. The smell of piss stings my nose as I tiptoe around fried chicken bones and used condoms.

Why are the streets so deserted? I see a couple

of mums with buggies but that's about it. I pass a basketball court covered in graffiti and surrounded by railings, empty but for the crisp packets that chase around its scuffed surface. Rubbish spills out of bins, and someone has dumped a dirty mattress up against a wall. The whole estate is as trashed as I feel.

A block stands empty, ready to be torn down. Some of the windows are smashed and torn net curtains flap in the breeze. A forlorn "SAVE OUR HOMES" bed sheet is tied to a balcony.

Persephone House is the next block. It's just as tragic and I wonder if it's for the chop too. According to the letters, Marie lives at 6D Persephone House. There's an entry buzzer. I press 6D. It gives off a nasty honk and then crackles. I lean down and press my ear to the speaker. The crackle turns into a hiss.

"... is ... t?"

"Hello?" I say.

More hissing and crackling. "Wha ... want?"

"Is this the right address for Marie Beauvoir?" I ask.

"Who wants ... know?"

It's a girl but she doesn't sound like Marie. She has a Haitian accent – just like Grandma Beauvoir had.

"It's Samuel ... her nephew. This is the last address I had for her." There's a pause. "Hello?" I say again.

"She's ... a client ... come up ... wait."

Another honk and I hear the door click open.

The floor is littered with takeaway menus, leaves that have blown in and a shopping trolley. I'm not surprised the lift is out of order, and I'm not sure I'd have trusted it anyway. I find the stairs and it's six floors up. Of course it is. With a sigh, I start the climb.

The stairwell is dank, lit only by feeble, flickering lights. I see piles of dead flies at the bottom of each plastic case. I hear a baby wailing somewhere in the block, drowning out the throb of a bass-line. I wind my way up the stairs. I glance down the centre to see all the way to the ground floor and feel a sudden rush of vertigo in my gut.

I'm glad when I turn a corner and see the door marked with a faded "6". I head down the corridor towards 6D. 6B is sealed shut with police tape and the entire hall reeks of strong skunk. I am sad Aunt Marie lives here.

The door of 6D opens an inch and a wave of incense hits me. My head fills with fog. A beautiful eye peers through the crack. "What do you want?" a voice says. It's the same girl who answered the buzzer.

"Just to see my aunt," I say.

"She busy."

"But she's here? I can wait."

The door closes and the chain is slid off. The door opens a little wider and there stands a petite girl about my age with huge doe eyes and full lips, her black hair worn natural. "Come in. I don't know how long she be."

She steps aside so I can enter. A boxy hall opens

into a cluttered front room. Blood red and purple shawls are tacked over the windows, letting in precious little daylight. There's not much furniture, it's more like a shrine – candles burn and dribble, lit for statues and icons of gods. Most of them look like saints and the Madonna, but it's unlike any church I've ever seen. Perhaps that's because of the human skulls that grin on shelves and the cage of hens that cluck in the corner.

There are books and beads, and bundles of lavender and sage hang from the ceiling. There's a bookcase of items for sale – candles for love, potions to forget your love, candles for healing, potions to cause harm.

I knew it. Somehow I knew it, but now I've seen it with my own eyes. There was only one thing that would cause my father to reject his only sister. To him, religion is thicker than blood.

A beaded curtain parts and an old women hobbles in, leaning on a cane. "May God bless you richly, Madame Beauvoir."

"Whatchya be talkin' about, Edna?" a voice booms from the other side of the curtain in an extravagant accent. "We prayin' for you, chil'."

Marie appears behind Edna and she's just as I remember her, perhaps a little more hefty in middle age, a little more buxom. Her hair is in bantu knots, and her gold metallic dress is big as a tent. Big hooped earrings swing around her face like wrecking balls.

"Madame Beauvoir, you are a true angel. An angel on earth."

"Ah, hush ya mouth, ya make an old woman blush!"

What is with that accent? Then her gaze falls on me and her eyes widen. She steers Edna to the door.

"You keep a-takin' de 'erb an' root, chil', and I see ya next week a de same time. Antoinette help ya to de lift." She almost shoves the old woman out of the room, shooing Antoinette after her.

"Oh my days," she says the second the door is

shut. Her voice is back to her normal South London accent. "You cannot be Samuel Beauvoir, because if this handsome bastard what stands before me is my nephew, I must be a hundred years old."

I smile and she throws her arms around me. Her bear-hug takes my breath away.

"What's with the accent?" I ask.

She lets go of me and shrugs. "Hoodoo Priestess innit."

It's strange – I feel better than I have since the accident. Just being close to Marie stokes the coals in my chest. "It's good to see you," I say.

"How is my fool brother? He send you?" Her head tips to the side. "No, it's something else, ain't it?"

I nod as Antoinette comes back into the flat. She offers to take my coat and I hand it over.

"OK, you better come in then. Antoinette, put the kettle on, yeah?"

Antoinette ducks behind a brocade curtain hiding, I assume, the kitchen.

Marie holds the beads aside and hustles me in. The bedroom has been converted into some sort of fortune-teller's caravan. There's a table in the centre, with candles glimmering all around. On the table rests a deck of tarot cards and a bronze bowl, inside which something is still smoking. The room smells strange, a little eggy, and the air feels like treacle.

"Sit yourself down, hon."

There's a velvet 'throne', but I'm pretty sure that's for Marie.

"Dad's fine," I tell her. "You know Dad. He never changes, does he?"

"Oh he's a rock of ages all right." Marie takes her seat and her sadness is clear.

"Is this what you fell out about?" I ask.

"Oh yes," she says. "Didn't like me working the root one little bit. Never did. He don't like reminding of where he comes from, of who he is."

"Was Grandma ...?"

"Yep."

34

I nod. We fall silent. After so many years apart, what is there to talk about? The weather?

"But you're not here to talk about your dear old dad, are you?" Marie looks at me. "No ... this is about you. Sam, I can feel it coming off you in waves. It's like tar."

"What is?"

"Grief. Anger. Guilt. Despair. Son, it's some dark matter you got up in there." She taps her head. I believe her in a way I don't believe Dad. I believe she can read me. "It's a girl, ain't it?"

It's like a punch in the gut. Tears burn my eyes. I take a deep, long breath, try to hold them in.

"Son, we don't judge here. You let it out."

I nod. "I'm OK. Yeah. It's a girl. My girlfriend, Eliza. She died."

"Oh, Samuel. I'm so sorry." Marie takes hold of my hands and closes her eyes. I feel the toasty warmth of the car heater on my feet and I see it all again.

It shouldn't have happened. We were supposed to turn left at the junction, but the Range Rover coming downhill swooped into our path. I know how to skid ... you turn into it, but it just didn't work. As I swerved to get out of the Range Rover's way, I lost control. Eliza screamed my name. I saw her grip the door to brace herself. I felt the floor drop away as we left the road and rolled down the verge. I didn't know which way was up and which was down.

And then, the impact with the trees. The windscreen shattered. The airbag hit my face. I passed out – but only for a second. I knew I had to wake up for Eliza.

I don't remember getting us out of the car. My brain was a mess of adrenalin. Eliza's side of the car was crushed, but I got her free ... She was conscious. She asked me to pull her out. I laid her in the snow and, just when I thought we'd got away with it, I realised she couldn't breathe.

Eliza, can you hear me?

Samuel ...

Her eyes were glassy, looking into
the sky but not seeing it. Snow fell all
around us, oddly peaceful.

I'm here, I'm here.

I took Eliza's frozen hand
in mine. Her breath came
in horrid, wet rasps.
Blood bubbled on her
pale lips.

Don't let me go.

I won't.

She gripped my hand.

Please, Samuel ...

I promise I won't. I won't let you go.

Her grip went slack.

"Oh you poor thing!" Marie says as she drops my hand and the memory fades. "I'm so sorry."

I don't know what to say.

"Listen. You mustn't blame yourself. It wasn't no one's fault, it was an accident."

"Maybe ... maybe I shouldn't have moved her," I say.

"Stop that right now, hon." Her voice is stern. "You did what you thought was right. You was tryin' to save her. She'd have done the same."

I shake my head. Whatever Marie says, I know it was my fault. I was driving. We should have stayed at Fish's house. I *insisted* that we went out in that terrible weather. I killed Eliza.

And now I'll bring her back.

Marie springs up and rummages in a cupboard in the corner. "Well, my boy," she declares. "You've come to the right place. I'm gonna knock you up something that's gonna help you sleep and something that's gonna help you relax." Her bum sticks up in the air as she roots around on her hands and knees. "What you need is time, Samuel. Yeah, I know it's a cliché, but it will get better in time. Until it does, this'll keep you calm and level, yeah?"

"No," I say. "That's not what I came for."

Marie backs out of the cupboard and gets to her feet. "What do you mean?"

I wipe my hands on my jeans. "Can you remember that time in the garden? With the sparrow?"

Marie frowns for a second. "Oh, Samuel, no. No, baby."

"Can you do it?" I ask.

Marie's lips go tight. "Is that what you think I am?"

"Well, isn't it?"

"No, it bloody well isn't!" she almost shouts. "Because I work the root, you think I can raise the dead? You crazy if you think that!"

"But the bird ..."

"I healed the bird!" she cries. "It wasn't dead. We was connected and so I lent it some of my strength and the strength of the spirits too. That's all it was, Samuel, that's what I do. It's all connected – the earth, the trees, the insects and the animals – it's all one thing. I just pass the luck around."

I pause for a second, and what she's said sinks in. "But you *could* do it? If you wanted to?"

Marie slams her hand hard on the table and the bowl tips. "But I do not want! We do *not* interfere with death. Ever! I deal in luck, not life."

"Please, Aunt Marie, I beg you," I say, and I reach for her hand. "You didn't know Eliza ... She was this ... just *amazing* person. She didn't deserve to die."

"You think there's people who *do* deserve to die?"

Aunt Marie shakes her head. "What would your dad say if he could hear this?"

"I don't care! I just want Eliza back!"

The candles cast shadows over Marie's face. "The dead belong in the spirit world, Samuel," she says, so disappointed in me. "We all meet Papa Legba in the end, and you better believe he guards the crossing closely."

"But what about zombies?"

"What *Dawn of the Walkin' Dead* claptrap you been fillin' yer head with? That what you want? A zombie girlfriend?" Marie takes a deep breath. "You don't mess with death, Samuel. It's the one thing we got in common ... rich or poor, black or white ... we all get the same end. It gives life its balance and without balance ... well, it don't bear thinkin' about. We might work the root, but we keep the balance. We give as much as we take. Always."

Marie isn't going to help me. This is a waste of time. "It's not fair," I whisper.

"Both me and your dad would be out of work if life was fair."

"She was seventeen." A tear rolls down my cheek.

Marie embraces me for a moment then wipes the tear away. "Mix these as a tea to help you sleep," she says as she presses a bag of herbs into my hands. "And this to relax. Best you don't tell your dad we met. I'll keep you and Eliza in my prayers. I'll pray for her safe crossing, and you … you need to let her go. She's with the Loa spirits now."

"I'm gonna go," I say, my voice thin.

"I think that's a good idea."

I push my way out of the bead curtain. Antoinette hovers outside. Marie shows me to the door. "Look, Sam, I don't blame you for tryin' yeah?" she says. "It's only human. That's the most human thing there is, but leave the spirits well alone, you hear me?"

All I can do is nod.

"Now. Next time, you call me before you come,

like a normal person, and we'll go down Nando's, yeah?"

I manage a dry laugh. "Yeah. That sounds good," I lie. I won't come back. How can I? What must she think of me?

Aunt Marie kisses me goodbye on both cheeks and I slope to the stairs, not aware of the heady mix of smells any more. I start down the steps.

"Samuel!" a voice calls from above. Antoinette chases after me. "You forgot your gloves."

I pat my pockets, where I thought I'd put them. They're gone. I head back up the stairs and meet her half way. As she puts them in my hand, I feel a scrap of paper on my palm. Antoinette leans in close, like she's about to kiss me. She speaks in the ghost of a whisper.

"What choo need is da Milk Man."

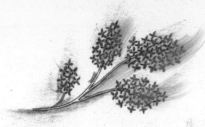

5

Chelsea is harder to get to than Brixton and the address Antoinette gave me doesn't show up on Google Maps. It seems there's no such place as Old Lived Passage off the King's Road. But I can take the bus to the King's Road and find it from there.

I sit on the top deck of the 345 to South Kensington, my stomach churning. A can of Red Bull rolls up and down the aisle every time the bus driver brakes. Antoinette said no more, just gave me the scrap of paper and darted back up the stairs. All I have is an address. I think she heard every last word I said to Aunt Marie – the intensity in her eyes told me as much. But I don't know why she's helping me.

I don't even know who she is. I feel like I'm doing something wrong, dipping my fingers into something thick and oily.

I get off at the King's Road and turn left. The air is muggy, the sky is the colour of a fresh bruise and I wonder if it might rain. Chelsea is a world away from Brixton and I feel very black again.

I pass the Bluebird Café, looking for somewhere that might be Old Lived Passage. But the King's Road is long, and I soon realise it'll take me all day without Google Maps. I could be walking totally the wrong way.

It starts to rain. Brilliant. A thick splatter lands on my cheek and I think I should abandon my search before the heavens open. A bus passes too close to the kerb and its wing mirror almost takes me out. I curse, but as the bus sails past, I spot a narrow alley between a coffee shop and a fancy boutique on the other side of the road. Sure enough, the rusty sign reads "Old Lived Passage SW3". I've found it.

I dart over the road, just avoiding a black cab, and duck down the alley. It's cold, dark and dank, smelling of earth and that rainy, static charge that follows a storm. The slabs, cracked and uneven, lead to a single door at the end of the alley. Blood red paint peels from the frame, and the knocker – a brass hand holding an orb – is grimy. There is no sign – for all I know this is someone's house.

I reach for the knocker and give three curt raps. I curse and wonder if Antoinette has sent me on a wild goose chase. I'm about to turn away when I hear footsteps shuffle to the door. It opens with a creak and a hunched old woman peeks through the gap. She has a white stick and round, bug-like shades cover her eyes.

"Oh hello," I say. "I hope this is the right address. I'm looking for ..."

"*Da ... da ...*" she says in what I think is a Russian accent. "Yes. You are expected." She stands aside and ushers me in. Antoinette must have called ahead.

"Oh my ..." I can't help but gasp. I step into a vast lobby. The entrance is tatty, but my jaw drops as I take in the grandeur beyond. It's incredible. The floor is tiled like a vast chessboard. It plays tricks on my eyes as it stretches towards a deep stone fireplace.

Around the blazing fire are a sofa, chaise longue and armchair, all in the same jade green. The old woman gestures at them.

"Sit ... you sit ..." she says, with a kind but dotty half-smile. Three steps lead down from the hall. Tall, arched windows loom over the room like a mountain range, but let in scant light. Instead, candles flicker from candelabras and their waxy stalactites drip to the floor.

A silver tea service sits on a low table, and steam winds from the teapot spout. Two china cups wait on saucers. Feeling stiff and out of place, I perch in the armchair and fold my hands in my lap. Up close, the fire gives off a powerful wall of heat.

I don't even know who it is I'm here to see. What sort of a name is Milk Man, anyway?

"Excuse me …" I crane to look for her, but the old lady is nowhere to be seen.

When I turn back to the fire, a man is leaning elegantly against the stone fireplace, as if he's always been there. I'm so surprised I flinch back into the chair. "Oh my … I didn't hear you!" I sound like a fool, and probably look it too.

But I now understand "Milk Man".

He is albino. His skin is snow white as is his hair. It falls down his back to his waist as fine as spider's silk. Spiky white lashes frame his violet-pink eyes. I'm not attracted to him like *that*, but he's *beautiful*, like a perfect statue carved in chalky marble. His thin body is all angles, and he's dressed in a dapper grey suit and crisp white shirt. His black shoes are so polished they shine like mirrors.

"Samuel Beauvoir, I assume."

"Yes. Yes, that's me. And you're …?"

"They call me the Milk Man. It's as good a name as any other I've had, I suppose." His voice is deep but soft – melodic like a song. Between his soothing voice and the crackling fire, I could so easily fall asleep.

"I don't mean to sound rude," I say, "but who are you?"

"A friend. A mutual friend of ours told me of your need."

"Antoinette?"

"Yes. I know what it is you want, Samuel."

"Eliza," I say, cutting to the chase. "You can bring her back?"

The Milk Man glides over to the chaise longue and sits, crossing one long leg over the other. "I," he says with a cat-like smile, "am a facilitator. A middle man. I can *empower* you to bring Miss Grey back. But only if you're willing to make the necessary sacrifices."

I sit on the edge of my seat. "Anything," I tell him. "I'll do whatever it takes."

"That, my dear boy, is what they all say, but

so few see it to the bitter end. In truth, do you understand what you're entering into?"

I fumble my words. "I ... I don't know ... I just know it's not fair that Eliza died. If there's a way ..."

"There is a way," he says, idly inspecting his nails. "But it isn't easy and there's always a price. Allow me to tell you about myself, Samuel. I'm a pupil of the universe. Bathsheba and I have travelled the four corners of the world, learning and listening as we go. I've seen things that would exceed your wildest dreams and your worst nightmares."

He pauses to pour the tea. "Milk?" he asks, almost sarcastically.

"Please."

"As I was saying, on my travels I met a great deal of ... fascinating people. Vodun, voodoo and hoodoo have spread all around the world, Samuel. A lot of people *claim* to understand the power, but I've *seen* it. I've seen what can be done. Did you know, after a person dies, their spirit is trapped between this world

The Milk Man

and the next for a year and a day? Some people believe a soul lives like a guardian angel – they leave offerings for it at trees or rocks, but under certain circumstances the spirit can be called back to the realm of flesh."

"What circumstances?" I say. "I'll do it."

The Milk Man takes a sip from his cup. I see that he takes his own tea black. "First let us discuss the price."

"How much?" I blurt, with more force than I intend.

This time he smiles a much wider smile, like a shark's. "Oh Samuel, it's not as crass as that. You have to understand – the first rule of vodun is balance. All energy is connected. If one drinks greedily from one pool, a thirst is keenly felt in another. Where there is life there must also be death – for every gift a sacrifice. In this case, *you* must give of yourself for Eliza's return."

"Me or her? Her, every time," I insist. "If I have to die ..."

The Milk Man holds up an elegant hand to stop me. "There's really no call for *that*. You don't have to die, but the process won't be painless."

"I can't be in more pain than I already am," I tell him.

"Oh, how poetic," he says. "I have in my possession instructions for a ceremony. If you follow them to the letter, Eliza will be returned to you."

Aunt Marie's warning echoes around the grand hall. "And she'll be ... normal?" I say. "Not a zombie?"

He tuts. "What *have* you been watching, Samuel? No, she'll be your Eliza."

I nod. "So can I have the instructions? Please."

"Of course." He smiles. "I'm happy to help. Oh, there's the petty matter of my administration fee. The *cost* is on your conscience, but I do take a little something extra for my time and effort."

I stop myself rolling my eyes. Of *course* there's a fee. "And how much is that little something?"

The Milk Man keeps his eyes on mine as he picks

up a pad of cream paper and produces a fountain pen from his pocket. He scribbles a number down and hands me the pad. I blink and look up at him.

"Are you serious?"

"The question is, Samuel, are *you*?" he asks with a smile. I swear he bats his eyelashes.

The figure is the exact amount of money I have in my savings account.

"Silly me, I must have been mistaken." His tone shifts. "There *I* was thinking you wanted to bring someone *back from the dead*. Do you think it's child's play, Samuel? If it was cheap, we'd all be at it."

I shake my head. What the hell. I can't imagine *any* future without Eliza, so what difference does a few thousand pounds make? I can earn more money, but there'll never be another Eliza. "OK."

"Wonderful." The Milk Man reaches inside his pocket again, this time for a crisp white envelope.

"Is that the instructions?"

"No, dear boy," he tells me. "That's my bank

details. As soon as I have the money you'll receive
my instructions."

"Oh. OK."

He waves a delicate hand as light as lace at the
door. "It's been a delight, dear Samuel. Now – be
sure before you begin. It'll change you for ever.
Be sure."

"I am sure."

"Very well. It was an absolute pleasure to do
business with you."

Bathsheba is at the door, ready to show me out.
She bows and nods, meek as a mouse. I turn to shake
the Milk Man's hand, but he has gone, absorbed into
the shadows.

"Thanks," I say to no one in particular and step
out into the alley.

The rain has stopped. How odd. I'm sure I was
inside for only a few minutes, but now night is
creeping in.

6

I'm at the kitchen table with my laptop listening to the rain rat-a-tat at the window. I'm all set to transfer every penny I have to Milk Man's account. As I click on "confirm", the doorbell rings.

Mother is doing her yoga in the lounge. "Samuel, darling, can you get that?" she calls.

I say nothing but pad down the gloomy hall to the front door. I open it to find a leather-clad motorbike messenger on the step. The rain bounces off his black helmet, the visor down all the way. Without a word, he hands me a package. The spidery italics on the address label are now smeared by rain.

I take it and the biker melts back into the night.

"Who is it?" Mum calls.

"Erm ... Jehovah's Witnesses."

"Oh for goodness sake! We live at the rectory!"

"That's what I told them," I say. "I'll be up in my room."

"I'll be done in ten if you want to watch the next episode of *The Danish Murder* or whatever it's called."

I manage a chuckle, but I'm already half way up the stairs. I lock my bedroom door and flick the lamp on. The Milk Man was true to his word. I tear open the package and find a notebook bound in scarlet leather.

The writing is in the same curling script as the address.

The first page is a title – *To Return A Soul Lost*.

I turn the page and see a warning – *The user understands not all that is lost can be found and that balance must be restored.*

OK, I get all that. Impatient, I turn to the next page.

TO RESTORE A SOUL

1. In a bowl of clay mix the following.

    Two teaspoons of clove oil, frankincense oil
    and yellow camphor oil.

    A small chunk of benzoin resin.

    A lock of the dead man's hair.

    A pint of goat's blood. The blood MUST be
    warm and fresh.

    A pinch of dirt from the dead man's grave.

    A tooth from a loved one.

    One moth, alive.

    Petals taken from the dead man's favourite
    flower.

2. Start with the oils and warm the ingredients over
    a red candle. Stir gently, anti-clockwise, with a
    wooden spoon until they form a single solution.
    Grind the solids into a fine powder, then add to
    the mix.

3. *Pour the solution into a small shell – that of a snail, crab or small turtle.*

4. *Place the shell on the dead man's tongue.*

5. *Stitch shut the dead man's lips to seal the soul within.*

6. *Bury the dead man before the clock strikes midnight. Consecrate the grave with holy water.*

I read the instructions, then read them again, and again.

My heart sinks. I never expected it to be easy, and I know that hoodoo rituals often ask for natural ingredients. It could have been *far* worse, to be honest. The internet will help with most of the items, but Eliza's hair? The tooth of a loved one? And where will I get fresh goat's blood from? I shudder. I'd give my own if I could, but that's not what the ritual asks for.

I slide off my bed and sit on the floor. I feel nauseous and light-headed. Can I do this? Can I dig her up and ... tamper with her body? I want to be strong but I don't know if I can ... it's ... ghoulish.

I get it. I'm being tested. The Milk Man said nothing comes for free and I have to pay if I want Eliza back. If it works, it'll all be worth it. If it doesn't ... well, at least I can say I did *everything*.

I have to try. If I don't, I'll wonder about it for ever. I'll never be able to rest. The Milk Man said she would be *my* Eliza. Everything can go back to how it was before the crash.

I feel crushed by tiredness. I look to the clock – it's just after nine. If my body was willing, I'd make a start right now, but I don't think I can. No. I will rest and start afresh in the morning.

7

I have no intention of going to school today, but I at least put on my uniform and make my way to Eliza's house as soon as the clock strikes eight. From the driveway, I see the windows are stuffed with a macabre jungle of white lilies and orchids – the flowers of death. I can't imagine her mother will have gone back to work yet, but I'm here before nine anyway.

I knock on the door and Mrs Grey answers. She looks washed out and gaunt, in a drab dressing gown.

"Oh Samuel," she says and I sense I've woken her. "What time is it?"

"I'm on my way to school," I lie. "Mum is making me go back today."

"That's for the best," she says, as she wakes up a little. "It's your final year after all."

"This is awkward," I begin, "but the last time I was here … me and … we were studying together and I left my textbooks in Eliza's room."

Mrs Grey welcomes me into the hall. "Oh, it's not awkward at all. Go on up, Sam. We haven't … we haven't even started to think about her things yet."

"Thank you," I say, and I head upstairs. I'm thankful that Mrs Grey doesn't follow. This house is so familiar, but now it feels like all the colour has drained out of it. I feel like I'm wading through a sunken shipwreck.

I pass Eliza's brother's room. I can hear him getting ready for school as I slip into Eliza's room. It's true – they haven't touched anything. It's like a snapshot of her final day – her bed is unmade, a denim skirt and a pair of electric blue tights are flung on the duvet. I remember how she chose to wear jeans instead – because it was so cold. I drift around the room like a phantom, my fingers graze the window sill, her teddy bear, her dressing table. I remember waiting on the drive, honking the horn to let her know I'd arrived. A little tin of Vaseline lies on the dressing table, lid off. She must have tossed it there as she rushed down to me.

And next to that is a hairbrush. I snatch it up and shove it into my rucksack, then I see her Sociology textbook poking out from under her bed. I pick it up to cover my lie. A copy of *Dracula*, our English set text, is open on her bedside table. I hope she'll get to finish it. Next to the book is a framed photo of us – in fancy dress last summer. I pick it up and smile. It was an "S Party" for Shaun Solomon's birthday. I went as Superman. Eliza, brilliant as ever, went as a squid.

I leave her room and walk slap-bang into Jake, her little brother. "Oh. Hi, Sam. What are you doing here?"

"I just needed this," I say, holding up the textbook.

"Cool. See you at school, yeah."

"Yeah." As he turns to leave I add, "Jake?"

"Yeah?"

"Did you ... erm ... keep any of your baby teeth from when you were little?"

He looks at me in horror. "Ew. No. Why?"

"Oh. Science experiment. Teeth and fizzy drinks or something."

He doesn't look any less horrified. Fair enough. "OK. No. Sorry, dude. Maybe try a dentist?"

"Cool, good call." If only it were that simple.

I leave Eliza's and head to the town library. I'm in the sixth form, so I'm allowed off school grounds – everyone knows we have study periods.

I find a quiet corner of the computer room and google the less extreme ingredients. It turns out the clove, frankincense and camphor oils, and the benzoin resin, are all used in perfumes and shouldn't be too hard to buy online. If only I hadn't just spent every last penny I had on the actual recipe.

A wicked idea pops into my mind. At home, the computer has helpfully stored Mum and Dad's credit card details. I find a store that does next-day delivery for an extra £5. Good, I can't wait. Yes, the Milk Man said a year and a day, but with every minute that passes it feels like Eliza's soul drifts on a tide, further and further out into the afterlife.

If only I could get the rest of the ingredients at the click of a mouse. I know what I have to do next and dark, horrible plans are forming in my head.

8

The next evening, as dusk thickens, I go to Eliza's grave. Atop it, the dirt is still piled in a fresh heap. I scoop some into a plastic bag and seal it.

The goat is going to be much harder. Mr and Mrs Bogart, two of the most devoted of Dad's church-goers, keep a small zoo of animals. It's part of their quest to be self-sufficient – five minutes away from Waitrose. As night falls, I lurk close to their house. The lights are all out – neither of them is back from work yet. I check the coast is clear, then I slip around the side and into the back garden. When I was little, if both Mother and Father were working and Mrs Fanshaw was busy, I was sent to Mr and Mrs

Bogart's, so I remember the layout. The chicken coop is next to the vegetable patch and the goats are kept in a shelter well away from anything they might eat.

There are two goats – kept for their milk and to trim the grass. As I approach, they both spring to their feet and tap-dance to and fro over their hay.

"Shhhh," I say as they start to bleat.

I haven't got time for guilt. It feels like my heart is full of gravel but I have to remember that it's just a goat. It's an *animal* ... and I'm not even vegetarian.

Yeah, but Eliza was ...

I elbow that thought out of my head. One goat is a small price to pay.

Thick leather straps – no doubt chew-proof – tether both goats to a steel rod. I grab the pole and pull on it, hard. My arm muscles strain but I yank it loose. I free the straps and let the pole fall. I grab at the closest strap, unwilling to choose between the two goats. I leave the other to roam free – it flees over the lawn to the vegetable patch – and keep a hold of the other.

It huffs and tugs on its lead, like it *knows*.

"Shhhh!" I urge.

The rectory is just around the corner and so I can tramp through the trees at the back of the houses rather than take the road. With any luck, I won't be seen. I fall a couple of times, skinning my knees through my jeans, but manage to drag the goat to our garden. I make sure we're far enough away from the back door and tie the strap to a thick root. I can't bring myself to look the poor goat in the eye. This must be why hangmen wear hoods.

I only hope Mr and Mrs Bogart don't think to search the trees when they discover their goats have "escaped".

I leave the goat and open the back door into the kitchen. "Mum? Dad? Mrs Fanshaw?" I call. No reply. Good. I'm making muddy footprints all over the tiles, but I don't care. I take a kitchen knife from the block and a big glass jug from the cupboard.

I turn away from the mirror by the back door. I can't even face *myself* as I head back into the garden.

When I return to the kitchen, I am covered in blood, dazed and out of breath. I hadn't expected it to spray from the goat like that. I must have hit an artery. I put the jug on the counter and peel my jeans and hoodie off. They're beyond cleaning. I'll have to bury them with what's left of the goat. I strip to my boxer shorts and shove everything into a black bag.

At the sink, I scrub and scrub at my hands until my skin is sore, watching pink water gurgle away with washing-up bubbles. I'm not sure I'll feel clean ever again. I feel like Lady MacBeth. *Out, damned spot*.

I bend down and wince as I'm reminded of my skinned knees. I root in the cupboards until I find what I'm looking for – a Moroccan pot we never, ever use. It's the closest thing to a clay bowl we have.

I wipe any tell-tale drops of goat blood off the counter, then hurry upstairs with the jug and the pot. I'm still alone in the house. I think Dad has a Bible study group tonight and I have no idea where Mum is. The box with the ingredients from the chemist is on my bed – it arrived this afternoon.

Everything is ready in the centre of my floor. I've cleared all the furniture to one side. The candle burns. There's only one ingredient left.

I go to the bathroom. On the side of the sink are some anaesthetic cream and a pair of pliers from Father's tool kit.

In the mirror, my face is stony. I stare into my eyes, trying to psych myself up. I've given it some thought and I'm guessing a front tooth, one of the little ones on the bottom row, will be easier to extract than the teeth with roots at the back.

I grip the sink and take deep breaths.

I rub the anaesthetic on my gums at the front and back. It stings, then it tingles, then it just feels warm.

Nothing comes for free. Prove you're worthy. Pay the price.

I pick up the pliers.

I clean the blood out of the sink, press cotton wool into the wound, then return to my room. The tooth is in my hand. The bottom half of my face is bloated and swollen. I'm in agony. I've taken three painkillers and I just hope they kick in soon. My breath is unsteady and I can taste blood on my tongue. People always say blood tastes like copper and they're right.

I've made a stove out of four red bricks and a candle. While the oils heat over the flame, I grind the tooth and hair and lilac petals with a pestle and mortar I found in the kitchen. The tooth crumbles, but the hair is more of a challenge – it flakes into stubborn fibres.

At last I have a substance like sand, which I add to the mixture along with the goat's blood. Next, I unscrew the lid from the old jam jar that holds a frantic moth hostage and drop it in. Its lacy wings flutter as it struggles before being sucked under the surface.

I stir anti-clockwise and the red liquid soon turns as black as ink and as thick as glue. It bubbles. The final, awful shriek of the goat still rings in my ears. This better be worth it.

I look at my watch and it's almost half-nine now. I have to get to the graveyard before it's too late.

With the jam jar in one hand and a spade in the other, I stalk across the deserted graveyard. It's a freezing cold night and a silvery mist rolls between

the headstones. It makes finding Eliza's grave so
much harder.

On the one hand, the foggy tide will hide the
dreadful act I'm about to commit, but it also means I
won't see if anyone happens by. I daren't use a torch,
so I rely on the moonlight as I start to dig. Stone
angels gaze on, so very ashamed of me.

I knew it would be hard, but I didn't anticipate
how hard it would be to unearth Eliza. The plot is
bigger than I'd thought and the dirt I'm shifting just
rains back down unless I hurl each spadeful as far as
I can. Worse, the soil is frozen and hard-packed. It's
exhausting, and my shoulders burn with effort.

But I can't tire. If it takes too long, I'll be too late.
This has to be done before the witching hour. I drive
the spade deeper and deeper into the grave. After
what feels like hours, the metal of the spade clashes
with wood and I dig with fresh vigour. Before long,
I've cleared the soil around Eliza's coffin.

I stop.

I drop the spade. It clatters on her casket.

What am I doing?

I'm digging up my girlfriend's dead body.

What is *wrong* with me?

I close my eyes and remember our dance at the Year 11 Prom. Eliza looked so beautiful in her beaded ivory dress. The dress she was buried in. We danced the slow dance, our bodies pressed together, no room for air. Balloons fell from the ceiling and bounced around us. Her hair was curled into loose ringlets, and woven with tiny silk roses and pearls. "I love you," I whispered in her ear.

"People think we're too young to know what love feels like," Eliza said as she rested her head on my chest.

"And what do you think?"

"I think ... I think our hearts haven't been hurt yet so we love more freely. More playfully, with reckless abandon. I know I love you, Samuel, and I know you love me back."

I held her even closer.

Now I kneel on her coffin, my hands pressed to the cool, damp wood.

Eliza.

I won't waste another second. I spring to my feet, grab the spade and thrust it under the coffin lid. I force it open. I feel the nails give way, then cry out as I pull the lid to one side with the last bit of strength I have. I slip into the coffin next to her, exhausted.

Here she is.

I chose not to see her at the funeral home. I couldn't do it. I don't really want to see her now.

The body doesn't look like her. It looks like a waxwork model. Her skin is deathly white but covered with make-up – more make-up than she ever wore in life. The lilacs in her hands are brown and crisp and dead.

This is not Eliza.

I reach up out of the grave and pull my rucksack and the jam jar down with us.

I grimace as I tug her mouth open. Something cracks – they've wired her jaw shut. I have to force her lips apart. Dear God. I screw my eyes shut.

This is not Eliza.

From my rucksack I pull out a pretty little hermit crab shell. Mother found it on a beach years ago and put in the bathroom as a decoration. I didn't want to put something dirty and ugly in Eliza's mouth. I pour as much of the potion as I can into the shell, then place it gently at the back of Eliza's throat. I try to be careful, but a little spills over and black goo trickles over her pale cheek.

I clamp her cold, stiff lips together and reach for the sewing kit I brought from home.

I don't even realise I'm crying until my tears spatter on her face.

My arms feel like lead as I cast aside the spade and

flop down against the next-door headstone. Eliza's grave is a hump of freshly dug dirt. I've sloshed holy water over it, and it's a mess. She deserves so much better. I don't understand why I have to bury her if she's going to come back, but I don't dare defy the Milk Man's instructions.

I'm covered in sweat and dirt. I'm sure that I look and smell like what I am. A ghoul.

My guts turn without warning and I roll to one side to vomit. I haven't eaten for hours so I spew nothing but bitter bile. Exhausted, I fall back against the headstone.

What now?

I wait.

I listen.

If I hear so much as a murmur from under the earth, I'm digging her out. I can't stand the thought of Eliza, buried alive. I half expect her hand to shoot up out of the soil.

Nothing happens. My breath hangs in frozen

clouds. I pull my coat around me. I can't leave her. If she comes back, I need to be here to explain. I check my watch. It's still only ten to twelve. I did it in time, so why is nothing happening?

I'll wait until dawn if I have to.

The minutes crawl by. Midnight strikes and still no flicker of movement from the grave. Inside my hood, my face is numb with cold, my teeth clenched. I don't understand. I did everything I was told. Awful things. Did the Milk Man rip me off? Is he a charlatan, a con man? He certainly fooled me.

I cry. I'm too tired to stop myself. It's the first time I've let myself weep since the crash. Eliza has gone. I've lost her. Soon, my body is shaking with sobs and my cries echo in the graveyard. I feel as if I'm setting free some demon that's been trapped under my ribs. I let it go. I let her go.

I cry and cry until I'm drained. My eyelids go heavy and I lean back against a headstone.

I let myself fall asleep.

9

The first thing I hear is a steady *bleep bleep bleep*.
Morning light shines on my eyelids. I am warm. I'm
in a bed, the stiff sheets tucked under my arms. My
mouth is dry. All I can think is that someone must
have found me in the graveyard and taken me inside.
I wonder if I got hypothermia. Yes, that must be it.

I open my eyes and the light blinds me. I close
them again at once. Next, I open them a little at a
time, letting them adjust to the sunshine that burns
through the thin yellow curtains. I'm not at home.
Where am I?

I strain to sit up, but my body feels like wet clay.
I manage to lift my head to look towards my feet. My

vision is blurred, but I see an armchair at the foot of the bed. A girl is slumped in it, under a woollen blanket. A girl I'd recognise anywhere.

"Eliza?" My voice is hoarse.

She stirs. She lifts her head and pushes the blanket aside. "Sam?" She springs up and tumbles towards the bed. She swims into focus at my side. Her face is the best thing I've ever, ever seen. She leans close and rests a warm hand on my cheek. "You're awake! Oh God, which of these buttons is for the nurse?"

"You're alive," I mutter and she frowns.

"Of course I am! I'm right here. No, don't move. A nurse is on the way."

I try to cling to the sight of her, but I feel myself drift back to sleep. I pray this isn't a spiteful dream.

When I wake again, my head feels clearer. Now Eliza

is joined by Mother, Father and a woman I don't know. She looks young for a doctor, her hair in a messy bun on top of her head.

"Well, hello there, Samuel. My name is Dr Knight. Here, take a sip of water." She brings a beaker to my lips and I take a sip. My mouth feels like a desert.

"What's going on?" I croak.

"You were in a car crash last week," Dr Knight coos, her voice sweet and syrupy.

"No ... Eliza ..."

"I'm here, Sam." Eliza steps closer to the bed and takes my hand. She's solid, real. "Can you remember? I pulled you out of the car ... Can you remember – we skidded off the road in the snow?"

"You've been in a coma for the last six days, Sam," Dr Knight says. "We had to keep you there to reduce the pressure on your brain. How was the sleep? Sweet dreams?" she asks with a smile.

"Sleep?" I mutter. Can it be true? Has everything that's happened since the crash been a fever dream? Eliza. Aunt Marie. The Milk Man? It all felt so real, but at the same time the last few days have possessed the relentless forward-motion of a nightmare. I run my tongue over my bottom teeth. They're all there.

"Just rest, Samuel," Mother says. "You've suffered a lot."

"The whole church has been praying for you," Dad says. "You had us all worried there."

The tiredness is crushing me, making me feel drunk. I grip Eliza's hand. I'm never letting her go ever again.

10

Three days later, fully rested and recovered, I'm allowed to go home. It feels good to be out of the flimsy hospital gown and into real clothes. Eliza helps me pack my bag while Dad brings the car. I suspect I'll be wrapped in cotton wool for the next few months. Or years.

"God, I can't wait to see everyone again," I tell Eliza. "We should get them all together this weekend. Fish and Jade, Nick and Lewis, Zakiya and maybe Tom?"

Eliza stops what she's doing and zips up my hoodie for me. "Yeah, that sounds fun. Whatever you want."

"What do you want to do?"

"I don't mind. But we should take it easy. No booze. No driving. Maybe never again."

I kiss her tenderly on the lips. "I promise. What did I miss?"

She frowns, her nose wrinkles. "What do you mean?"

"Like, I was out of it for a week. Something must have happened! Are Jade and Fish off or on this week?"

Eliza shrugs. "I'm not sure. I ... I've been here all week. I didn't want to miss it if you woke up."

I wrap her in my arms and press her to my chest. "Aw, you're the best, you know that?"

"I never gave up on you, Sam. I knew you'd come back to me."

I don't know what's real and what's not, but I swear I can feel the invisible gold chains holding me and Eliza together. For ever.

"I know," I say. "I came back for you."

Which, either way, is true.

We arrive back home and Eliza is allowed to stay for the evening. I just want to be near her. I feel refreshed like my body has been flushed out with pure water. I'm very, very alive. I spring around the house, as full of energy as a daft puppy.

"Are you hungry?" I ask Eliza as she sips a cup of tea at the kitchen table.

"Not really," she says, "but I'll eat if you are."

The back door opens and Mother clatters in, swinging her big leather bag. She must have been on house visits. "Ooh, is that kettle on?" she says, then gives me a big kiss on the forehead. "How are you feeling, darling?"

"Fine! Like weirdly good!"

"That'll be a week of sleep," Mother says. "I could use that right now. I feel dreadful."

"What's wrong, Dr Beauvoir?" Eliza asks.

"Oh, Eliza, please call me Mel. It's been three years!"

"Sorry!"

"I feel terrible," Mum says. "Just when I thought my body's defences knew every last germ on earth, along comes a new one."

"I'm about to cook," I tell her. "Do you want something?"

"Samuel, you're an angel, but you should be taking it easy."

"I'm fine, honestly." I feel like I could run a marathon without breaking into a sweat.

"OK." Mum pulls off her shoes and tosses them aside. "There's a roast chicken in the fridge. You could have that with some salad or pasta or something."

Sounds good. While Mum makes a cup of tea, I head to the fridge and find the plate covered in foil.

"What do you think, Eliza? I could just do some fries –?"

I pull back the foil and drop the plate to the floor in disgust. I jerk back, smacking into the fridge door.

"Sam? Are you OK?" Mum asks.

"Ew! What's that?" Eliza gasps and covers her mouth with her hand.

The chicken is rotten, putrid. It stinks. Pearly white maggots squirm inside the slimy carcass on the floor. Brown liquid dribbles across the tiles.

"Oh my ..." Mum says.

"How long was it in there?" I say. I can't take my eyes off the wriggling maggots.

"Only since Sunday! I don't know how ... Dear God, it reeks!" Mum looks like she might vomit.

"I'll sort it ... and I'll clean the fridge too. Pizza?" I ask as I reach for the phone.

After Eliza has gone home, I sink into a too-hot bath. The sting of the water on my skin tells me I'm not dreaming. Steam swirls up past my eyes and I slide lower into the hot water. Now just my nose is above the surface.

It's uncanny, but *everyone* is so sure that I was the one injured in the crash. The days after Eliza died were a numb haze. Were they real? After all, how could some black oil and a crab shell re-write the last seven days around me? Impossible.

As I stew in the water, my eyelids become heavy.

I force my eyes open and I'm in the car, pinned against the steering wheel. A snowy branch juts into the window to my right. Freezing wind cuts through the car and powdery snow blows sideways. I hear Eliza call my name. The airbag deflates in my face.

"Sam, wake up!" she cries. "We have to get out of the car!"

She's leaning across the passenger seat and trying to haul me out. There's a graze on her face and a jewel of blood glistens in her hairline. She unclips my seatbelt and I struggle to get free. My left ankle feels weird, like it's bent over all wrong, and my knees throb.

"Can you hear me?" she says.

"Yeah," I say. My brain feels like it's come loose. It's swimming around in my skull. "I can't get out."

"And you can't go back," says a new, deep voice.

Instead of Eliza, the Milk Man sits calmly in the passenger seat. I shrink back, trying to get away.

The Milk Man smiles and his lips part. White spiders spill from his mouth, down his chin, over his chest, across his hair.

My head ducks under the water and I wake with a start. I struggle to sit up in the bath, making a splash. I don't quite feel alone. The water has gone tepid. It feels like unwanted hands touching me all over.

I don't know what's real or fantasy any more.

I get out of the bath and put a towel round my waist. I go to my room – there's only one thing I can think to try. I open my laptop and log into my online bank.

My fingers drum on my knee as I wait for the website to load my details. I click into my savings, holding my breath.

I don't know which option would be worse.

The balance is £0.00.

Bitter vomit floods my mouth but I swallow it back. It all really happened. I stagger and fall back onto my bed. As if to rub salt in my wounds, the Milk Man's little red notebook sits on my pillow. I don't remember leaving it there.

I wait until my hands stop shaking, then reach for it. Yes, what I did was awful, but I can't help but think it worked. This isn't exactly what I expected, but Eliza is back! She's alive! That was the reason for everything I did. Eliza is worth any sacrifice.

I flick to the last page of the Milk Man's book. There's a message I didn't see before, the words very small. Maybe I didn't *want* to see it. It reads –

Results may vary.

11

The Skate Park is the only cool place in town. Eliza and I don't skate, but most of our friends do. The ramps and pipes are outside so we mostly hang out on the sofas in the Skate Shop. It's a sort of coffee shop, sort of music venue, sort of hoodie store, sort of space for people to spray-paint their skateboards. It's also sort of the only place to go as half of us are still under-18s.

Fish and Jade are together this week, and they snuggle together on the battered leather sofa opposite me and Eliza.

"You look pretty good for a corpse," Fish jokes. He's called James Fisher, but he *does* look a bit like a catfish.

"Fish!" Jade gasps. Jade is famous for her pillow-like cleavage, which is on full display tonight. Her chest wobbles as she talks. "He almost died!"

"But he didn't! So it's fair game."

"I'll still kick your ass," I say with a smile as Zakiya joins us on the sofa.

"Oh my days!" she shouts as the DJ changes the track. "This is such a bop! Eliza, shall we dance?"

Eliza shakes her head. "I don't think so ... not right now."

"But this is a certified banger," says Zakiya. She's getting set to dance – fixing the brooch that holds her peacock blue hijab in place.

"I don't want to leave Sam," Eliza insists.

That's a bit weird. I don't want her to treat me like an invalid. "It's OK, babe, you can go dance if you want to."

Eliza's eyes widen. "But I don't want to. I want to be with you."

She's so earnest it's almost awkward. Her blue

eyes glaze over as if she's about to cry. I squeeze her close. I suppose it's understandable – in her mind, she almost lost me the way I lost her.

"Eliza, it's cool. I'm not going anywhere. I'm fine."

"Good." She snuggles into me. I see Jade and Zakiya share a confused look. I guess Eliza has suffered as I suffered, but now I have swapped our fates. I'm sure the clinginess won't last, it's very unlike her. From Day One we've been happy to let each other *be*. My girlfriend has her things and I have mine.

I look down at Eliza and see a plump bluebottle crawl over her pale cheek. She doesn't seem to notice, so I bat it away. She sits up. "What?"

"There … there was a fly on your cheek."

A new song starts – it's the one we slow-danced to at our prom.

"Oh well, now we *have* to dance," I say.

Eliza seems delighted. She grips my hand as I lead her to the dance floor. Jade and Zakiya are right

behind us. Fish guards the sofas with his life. I hold
Eliza close. I'm not much of a dancer, but I'm happy
to be with her. "Are you OK?" I ask.

"I am now," she says, her voice dreamy, like a
lullaby.

We drift in lazy circles. I'm in a kind of trance
until something strange snags my eye. I blink, not
sure if I'm imagining it. On the other side of the
dance floor, I see a black shape standing as still as
a statue. Couples twirl and dip around it. I stop
dancing. The person – if that's even what it is – is jet
black from head to toe, wet and glistening. It's like
it's been pulled from an oil slick. From here I can
only see its hunched, skeletal outline. It's horrible.
Why aren't people trying to get out of its way?

"Eliza? Can you see that ... thing?"

She turns and follows my pointed finger. "What?
What thing?"

The black shape turns, very slowly, and vanishes
into the crowd.

"That! There!"

"Babe, I don't know what you're pointing at. There's nothing there." Her expression changes from confusion to concern. "Sam, are you OK? Maybe we shouldn't have come out tonight. It's too soon."

I push past Zakiya and Jade, trying to find where the shape has gone.

"Oi!" Zakiya yells.

I duck and weave my way out of the crowd, scanning the room as I go, but I can't see the slimy … thing.

It's gone.

My heart feels full of the same black sludge. I have a horrible feeling that I'm the only one who saw the shape. A dark, rotten sense of dread creeps from my toes all the way up my spine.

I'm not sure that what I started is finished.

12

When I arrive home, the rectory slumbers, only a few lamps left on in the hall to guide me in. This is a tad weird, because it's not that late. The sideboard is packed with tacky Get Well Soon bouquets.

As I hang my coat up, Dad pokes his head out of his study. My hand flies to my chest in shock. I don't know why I'm so jumpy. "Good evening, Samuel."

"Hey. Where's Mum?"

"She's having an early night – she's not feeling very well."

"Oh, OK. What's wrong?"

"She says it's just the flu."

I suppose the grot she was feeling yesterday must have got worse.

"How are you, my boy?" Father asks.

I sigh. "God, I wish people would stop asking me that."

"That's a pound in the *Lord's Name In Vain* jar, please," he says, and I reach into my pocket. "We were worried, you know, Samuel," Father goes on. "I'm not surprised your mother feels run down after the stress of it all."

"I'm sorry ..."

"Hardly your fault. Accidents happen." He gives me a pat on the arm which is a grand gesture for him. "I felt it, you know. The Holy Spirit. I knew you were being protected. I prayed at your bedside and you were surrounded by a most brilliant light."

I shift, feeling uncomfortable. The Holy Spirit had nothing to do with what I did. "What if I'd died?" I ask.

"Samuel! What a terrible thing to say! Don't talk like that."

"No, but what if I had? What would you have done?" I want him to stop talking to me like I'm one of his wide-eyed Sunday School kids and tell me the truth. I want him to say he'd have lost his faith if I'd died. Or at least started to doubt God. Surely I'm worth that?

"I hope we'll never know." Father starts to head towards the stairs.

"Would you have blamed God?" I ask, louder than I intend.

He turns back to me. "No," he says. *"Trust in the Lord with all your heart* ... Proverbs 3, Samuel. It's not man's place to question God's plan, as hard as that may be sometimes. But on the darkest nights we have to look the hardest for light."

I'm too tired to argue. If it was part of God's great plan for Eliza to die, perhaps God also planned that I should bring her back.

Dad takes himself to bed, so I watch TV in the lounge.
I curl up on the sofa, half covered with a blanket.
There seems to be a chat show on every channel –
a famous person talking to a slightly *more* famous
person.

I scroll up the channels until I hear a host ask in
a chatty Irish accent, "So how does it feel to cheat
death?"

I sit up straight. The camera cuts back to reveal
Eliza and the Milk Man sitting together on a plush
red sofa. The Milk Man lolls like a panther. Eliza sits
next to him – her posture is stiff, her hands grasp her
knees. The Milk Man turns his head to stare down
the camera. He looks at me with a hungry smile.

I wake with a start and the dream blinks away.
When did I even fall asleep? I look at my phone –
it's 2.52 a.m. The TV screen now displays a message
telling me what time the channel will be back on air.

I hear floorboards creak above me. I wonder if
Dad is still awake or if Mum is restless. A tall shadow

sweeps across the fireplace – someone racing up the stairs. I push the blanket aside and turn the TV off.

"Father?" I whisper. There's no reply. 'How very strange,' I think. I wonder if I imagined it – I am sleepy.

I start up to bed, turning off lamps as I go.

As I tiptoe up the stairs, I become aware of a *rasp rasp rasp*. It's a ghastly noise – a throaty, breathless gurgle. I see that the door to Mum and Dad's room is ajar. I realise the sound is coming from there and I creep over on tiptoes. I peek around the door – Mum is alone in bed. The noise is her as she struggles to breathe. I guess Dad must be in the spare room.

Mum tosses and turns, tangled in the sheets. Her face is damp and shiny with sweat.

"Mum?" I ask, and I wonder if she needs me to bring her some water or medicine. She doesn't stir from her nightmare. I enter the room and cross to the bed. Shards of moonlight cut between a gap in the curtains and I see how pale and clammy she looks. "Mum? Can you hear me?" She still doesn't wake.

The hairs on the back of my neck bristle like someone is breathing on me. I know when I'm not alone in a room.

Very slowly, I turn back to the door. It's behind me – the same figure I saw in the Skate Shop. This time, the oily creature lurks in the corner between the wardrobe and the window.

It's in my home.

"What the –"

I stride over, ready to tackle it to the floor. I pounce on it and tumble against the wardrobe. In my arms is Dad's long black robe, nothing more. It's still attached to its wooden hanger.

Confused and embarrassed, I get to my feet and look over to check I haven't woken Mum. She's sleeping, her brow creased and her face damp. The same long shadow swoops across the bed from the landing. With the robe still heavy in my arms, I duck out of the room, but there's no one in sight.

I look back to Mum and feel stabbing pains in my gut. Only now do the Milk Man's words echo in my mind.

"Where there is life there must also be death – for every gift a sacrifice."

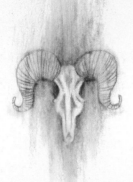

13

The next morning, Mum is even worse.

Dad summons the doctor, who tells him she's worried Mum has some kind of virus. If Dad can't get Mum to drink anything, it's possible she might have to go into hospital so she can be put on a drip.

I watch the exchange between Dad and the doctor play out from the side of the bedroom. I'm not at all sure this is a coincidence. The Milk Man said there'd be a price, but it was a price I thought I'd already paid. I think back to the screams of the goat as I took the knife to its neck, its eyes rolling in terror in its head. I took its life. I remember sewing Eliza's cold lips ...

I paid my price.

This is too much.

It's not fair.

Or maybe it is ... a life for a life.

I go back to my room and call Eliza. She answers straight away.

"Hey," I say. "I'm not going to school today."

"Oh." I can hear the disappointment in her voice. "Why?"

"I have to go back to the hospital," I lie. "For some check-ups."

"Can I come with you?"

"No, no it's cool. I'll be fine."

"I might not be," Eliza says. Her voice now has a hint of panic. "I miss you, Sam."

It's harsh, but I haven't got time for this. "Eliza, it's fine. I'll see you tonight, OK? Come over after school."

That seems to satisfy her. "Good," she says. "See you later. Take care, my love."

"You too. Love you."

"Love you *more*."

I know it's her voice, but she doesn't sound like Eliza. It's weird. I can only hope it'll pass when she knows I'm not at death's door.

I put my school uniform on, but head to the train station. I've taken some cash from Mum's purse to buy a ticket. I sit and fret all the way to Liverpool Street. Then I change for the Circle line to Sloane Square.

This time, I know exactly where to go and soon I'm at Old Lived Passage. The alley is dank, the air sharp with the smell of urine. Black rubbish sacks are dumped up against the wall, and I startle a mangy fox. The fox takes one look at me and flees, taking the remains of a KFC with him.

I step over the trash and hammer on the door. I

pause and listen for the shuffle of Bathsheba's feet.
But even with my ear pressed to the peeling paint, I
hear nothing. I give the handle a twist and the door
flops open.

A foul, fusty odour hits me like a brick wall. It
stinks. I hold my hand over my nose and fumble
into the gloomy hall. It's covered in litter – shopping
trolleys, a million take-out menus and *Evening
Standard*s, abandoned mattresses, old bins. The
handsome fireplace still stands in the middle of all
the rubbish, but wooden planks have been nailed over
the grand stained-glass windows. The *drip drip* of
leaks echoes in the hall. A rat skitters past my feet,
its tail as thick as my thumb.

Above the empty fireplace are the words – "NO
REFUNDS, NO GUARANTEES".

The message couldn't be any clearer.

It's even been written in white paint.

"Antoinette told me you'd be here," a voice behind
me says. My heart stops. It's Aunt Marie. She fills

the doorway in a furry leopard-print coat. "What have you gone and done, Samuel?"

"How did Antoinette know I'd be here?" I ask.

"I dread to think," Aunt Marie says. "She told me and left. Packed her stuff and walked out. Now, you wanna tell me what's going on, young man?"

I hang my head in shame.

"Cos it don't matter who I read any more," Marie says as she stalks towards me, kicking the junk aside. "All I see is you, boy, and a girl what shouldn't be here."

"It's not like that ..." I say. But it's exactly like that.

"She ain't got no business here, Sam, and neither does the thing that came back with her."

My heart drops like a pebble down a well. "What?"

"I seen it. That awful ... *thing*. You opened a door you shouldn't have opened, and Eliza's not the only thing that came back in from the cold."

"No ..." I cry.

Marie grabs my face and her cherry-red false nails dig into my cheeks. "Put it right, Sam!" she commands. "You get me? Put it right."

I realise I'm crying. I'm tired, so tired, and I'm losing my grip. "I can't, Aunt Marie. How can I?"

"You can, Samuel. That little boy I used to know knew right from wrong. And I ain't talking about breakin' the law, I'm talking about breaking the *natural laws*. Laws older than man." She's still talking right up in my face. "You messed with something *wrong*, Samuel, so now you gotta put it right."

I say nothing more, but bow my heavy head. I'm drowning. I know she's right. But I don't know what to do with the mess I've made.

Aunt Marie hands me a crumpled tissue from her handbag. "Dry your eyes, kid. Come on, let's get you home." She wraps an arm around me and it's the first solid, real thing I've felt since the crash.

14

I'm shattered by the time I walk in the front door of the rectory. Night is falling, but it feels like the sun hardly bothered to rise today.

"Hello?" I call, not too loud in case Mum is still resting. No reply. "Dad?" Still nothing.

All the flowers on the sideboard are wilted and brown. Dead petals litter the floor.

The house is bitterly cold.

"Samuel? Is that you?" It's Eliza. Her voice is coming from upstairs.

"Eliza?" I reply.

"I'm in your room."

I drag myself up the stairs and across the

shadowy landing. I feel heavier than a sack of stones. I flick the light switch, but the bulb must have blown.

Eliza stands before my window, looking up at the moon. Her hair glistens silver down her back. She turns to face me and I gasp. In the dull light, her face is gaunt and blue. Her eyes are hollow, dead, sunken, and crude stitches hold her lips together.

"Eliza ...?"

"What's wrong?" she asks.

I blink. Her face is back to normal. "Nothing ... I just ... nothing."

"I hope you don't mind," she says. "I let myself in. The back door was unlocked." She slips her arms around my neck and kisses my lips. Every inch of her skin is luminous in the darkness. She wears the night well.

"No, that's cool."

"How was the hospital?"

"What? Oh, yeah, it was fine."

"I missed you today."

"Did anything exciting happen?"

She looks up at me with half-closed eyes. "I don't know. I wasn't paying attention." She sighs and leads me to the bed. I lie down and she snuggles under my arm, rests her head on my chest. "Do you remember that day in Brighton?"

I smile. Best day ever. "Of course. Why?"

"I can't stop thinking about it – the seagull that pinched your chips, the crazy golf, that drunk woman who took our picture on the pier. It's all so clear in my head."

"I think watching the sun set into the sea was my favourite bit."

Her gaze is a million miles away. "It was so beautiful."

She's right. I remember every tiny detail. The sun was like a melting peach as it dissolved into the horizon and the sky burned hot pink. Eliza lay in my arms on the pebbles as we listened to the distant screams from the rollercoaster on the pier.

"What made you think of that?" I ask.

"I don't know," she says, nuzzling into me.

"Hey," I say. "Fish asked if we wanted to go over to his for a film ..."

"I want to stay here," Eliza says.

I wonder if she means we should lie here *all evening*. The landline rings. "I'd better get that in case Mum's asleep," I say and I untangle myself from Eliza and hurry to the hall. "Hello?"

"Thank goodness for that!" It's Dad. "Where on earth have you been? I've been calling and calling your mobile."

"Oh sorry, it must be on silent," I tell him. "Where are you?"

"I'm at the hospital."

"What?"

"It's your mum, Samuel. She's taken a turn for the worse."

It's as if the floor turns to quicksand under my feet. "Oh my G– ... is she OK?"

"No, no she isn't. Please come quick. Take Mum's car. Drive *very* carefully."

A vein throbs in my neck. I'm too hot. "I'll be there as fast as I can." I turn and recoil to see Eliza half way down the stairs. She moves so silently – I hadn't heard her at all.

"What's wrong?" she says.

"My mum is really ill. I have to drive to the hospital."

Her eyes widen. "I'll come with you."

"No!" I say, far too fast. "I mean ... this is just a family thing. Dad is really upset." She looks crushed – she wilts like the flowers dying on the sideboard. I know it's my fault, but I can't shake the feeling that all this is *because* of Eliza somehow. I don't want her anywhere near my mother. She's a bad penny, a rotten apple. "Sorry, Eliza. I have to go. You'll be fine. I'll call you from the hospital, I promise."

This seems to soothe Eliza. I drop her off at her house, then race to the hospital.

Dad's texted me the ward number and it doesn't take me long to find them in Intensive Care. The plastic corridors are washed out by icy lights. Staff in scrubs and masks dart about like ants. I find Dad outside a private room. He's pacing up and down, his jaw clenched.

"Dad, is she OK?" I ask.

"They're running some tests." He rubs his stubble. "They think it's some kind of virus, but they can't be sure. As we haven't been affected they think it's probably not contagious, but they're not taking any chances. At one point they asked if we'd visited West Africa recently."

I look at him in horror. "They think she has –"

I break off as a doctor and a nurse emerge from the private room. The doctor pulls her mask down so it hangs around her neck. "Reverend Beauvoir? Thank you for your patience. I'm Mrs Delaney, a consultant here. Your wife is stable for now, but we're still running tests. We are calling in an expert in tropical diseases. We'll also take a look at the records of your wife's patients. If I could have a minute, I'll talk you through her symptoms ..."

"Can I go in and see her?" I interrupt.

Delaney looks from me to the door. "Very well. But no physical contact, please, and don't remove the infection screen, whatever you do."

I nod and enter. It's bad. A transparent screen sits across Mum's bed, sealing off her upper body.

"Oh God, Mum ..." I pull up a chair and, against Delaney's instructions, hold her hand. Mum looks peaceful, but tubes run up her nose. In the low light, I see that they lead from a ventilator. They're helping her breathe. Never a good sign.

Her fingers curl around my hand.

"Mum?" I say.

Her eyes snap open. Wide open.

"Mum? It's OK, it's me, Sam."

She tries to say something, but I can't hear her over the ventilator.

"Don't try to talk. You're OK, Mum. You're in hospital." Her eyes widen further and she pushes herself up the bed, like she's trying to get away from me. She's terrified. The bleeps on her heart monitor get faster. "Mum, what is it?"

She lets go of my hand and points at me. Her finger trembles.

"It's just me!" I cry. "It's Sam!" I realise she's pointing *past* me. I twist around, but there's only a wall with a dull painting of a meadow, and a window. "Mum, what's wrong? Shall I get the doctor?"

But she's not pointing at me, she's pointing *past* me. She's pointing *up*.

I twist my head around slowly, because I *know*. I dare not breathe. The black thing is on the ceiling, crawling like a spider. I stumble and trip onto the bed. The dark shape hisses and scuttles to the darkest corner of the room. It has no way out.

I want to see it.

It's a *terrible* thing. It makes me feel every bad

feeling I've ever had all at the same time, but I still want to see it.

I feel sick.

I don't take my eyes off it as I get my phone from my pocket and flick the torch on. The beam swings onto the huddled shape. I see empty white eyes and a lipless mouth filled with teeth like needles. The next second, the shape becomes liquid and oozes like black ink into the air-con vent. The eyes and teeth are the last things to seep into the bars.

A shadow cuts across the window to the corridor and I wonder if it's the *thing*, but the handle goes down and Delaney enters the room with Dad.

"Samuel?" Dad asks. "Are you OK? Is your mum OK?"

I turn the torch off and shove the phone in my pocket. I look back to Mum and her eyes are closed. For now, at least, she can rest. She could see it. She could see it too.

Now I have no doubt. That thing is killing her.

15

I'm scared to leave Mum. No one else will see the black thing if it returns. There's a chair in the corner of the room. I'll sleep in that if I have to.

My phone rings. It's Eliza's landline and I realise I forgot to call her. I broke my promise. Dad glares at me.

"I'll take this outside."

I hurry out of the ward and hover near the doors, then I answer. "Hey, I'm sorry I didn't call –"

"Samuel?" A curt voice cuts me off. "It's Diana Grey. Is Eliza with you?"

I frown. "No. I dropped her off a couple of hours ago."

"Yes, I know, but she's gone again and didn't tell us where she was going. We thought she was up in her room."

I slide down the wall to squat on the floor. I'm not sure my head can take anything else today. "I bet she's come here to look for me. My mum's in the hospital."

A pause. "Oh ... I'm sorry to hear that. I do hope she's all right?"

"We ... we don't know yet. I'll call Eliza. I'll find her."

"Thank you, Samuel. Sorry to bother you."

I hang up and call Eliza. It goes straight to her voicemail and I feel a flutter of worry. I go to the reception desk and ask if a girl with long brown hair has come looking for me. The man at the desk tells me she has not. He checks with the front desk, but Eliza hasn't been there either.

I call Zakiya, unsure what else to do. I'm clutching at straws. "Hey, have you seen Eliza?" I ask, trying to keep the worry out of my voice.

"No. Not since school. Hey, Sam, is she OK? She's acting like, totally insane."

"She's fine," I snap. "She's fine," I repeat. I'm forcing myself to stay calm.

"Whatever. Maybe try the Skate Shop. I think Fish and Jade went there."

Damn! I don't want to leave Mum, but Eliza is acting ... differently ... and it's my fault. I have to find Eliza and bring her back to the hospital. It seems she can only find peace when we're together.

I text Dad an excuse and set off for the Skate Shop. It's band night and a girl with candy pink hair and black lips is singing like a sad ghost. She's doing little more than breathing into the microphone as a downbeat guitar strums along. It's not music to dance to and the crowd simply stands around the stage. I see Fish and Jade in the middle, his arm around her. They look happy, safe, together, and I realise that I'm none of these things.

I go up to the cute barista, Gabi. We come in so

often that I know her pretty well. She attends college on the other side of town. She's got blonde, messy hair and hip glasses. Her lips are letterbox red.

"Hey, Sam!" Gabi says. "How are you? Great to see you up and about."

"What? Oh yeah, I'm fine. Have you seen Eliza tonight?"

For a second Gabi looks baffled, and then sad. The band finishes a song and the crowd claps.

"Sam," Gabi says, her eyes wide. "Eliza died ... remember?"

My heart swells in my chest. "What did you say?"

"What?"

"What did you say?" I shout over the crowd.

Gabi holds her hands up. "Sam, relax! I just said I hadn't seen her since you were here together. Jeez. Can I get you some *decaf* maybe?"

"I'm sorry ... I thought you said something else."

I back away. What is going on? I need air. I push on a fire escape door and tumble into the night. The sky is endless and littered with stars. Eliza, so small in comparison, is lost out here somewhere.

I have to put this right.

But first I have to find her.

I drive home – I should have thought of this first – and run from room to room, but the rectory is dark, still and silent. It feels like no one has lived here in years and years. I sit on the bottom step, listening to the *tick-tock* of the clock. I can't spare these seconds, but I don't know what to do. I think about calling Eliza's parents to see if she's turned up, but if she hasn't that will only worry them. I text Dad to ask if she's at the hospital, but she's not.

I have no idea where else she'd be so I go back out and drive, just aimlessly roam the streets. I do a full loop of the town, slowing every time I see a female outline. God, I must look like a total pervert. I'm almost back home, when I see the spire of the church. But the view isn't right, and it takes me a second to figure out what's wrong.

Since when has there been a forest at the back of the church?

All that's ever been behind the church is the graveyard. The graveyard where we buried Eliza last week. I press down on the brake, slowing to get a better look. There's always been a few trees lining the path, but now it's rampantly overgrown, like it's been left to go wild for years.

I pull up in front of the gates, and park. The gates are locked at night. I could drive home and get the spare keys, but it's much quicker to climb over, the way the goths and glue-sniffers sometimes do.

The church grounds are never like this. The headstones tilt drunkenly, smothered with tall, feathery grasses, brambles, nettles and weeds. They look like rotten teeth jutting up out of the earth. I find what used to be the path, now covered in a carpet of moss. The angels, Madonnas and crosses are tangled in vines and creepers. Gnarly trees block out almost all the moonlight so I use the torch on my phone to light the way.

I get the horrible, crawling feeling that I'm being watched. I hear toads croaking and owls hooting. Fat, furry moths cluster around my phone. The air feels charged and I'm sure I see something slither under a decaying log.

As I pick my way through the forest, I hear a gentle, delicate sob, so quiet I almost miss it. It's Eliza.

I trample the marshy undergrowth, ignoring what's left of the path. "Eliza? Where are you?" I call. She doesn't reply, but her sobs become louder and harsher.

I see her. A column of pearly moonlight breaks through the canopy and Eliza is glowing. She's wearing her prom dress, her feet are bare and her hair hangs down her back. She's kneeling with her head bowed. Her shoulders shake with sobs.

"Eliza?" I slow, not wanting to scare her.

Then I see what she's
kneeling beside.

Here lies
ELIZA GREY
2000–2017

Beloved daughter
and sister

Rest in eternal peace

She turns to me.
"Sam," she says, as tears
run down her face. "I
died."

16

I fall to my knees next to Eliza. The ground is damp. I pull her close, and wrap my arms around her. "No ..."

"I did," she says. Her voice is barely a whisper. "You pulled me out of the car but I couldn't keep my eyes open. It was snowing. I was in your arms. I held your hand ... and then I left."

I cling to her. She smells of fresh lilacs.

"I don't know why I came here ... I just felt I had to," Eliza tells me. Her breath tickles my ear. "Sam, what did you do?"

I don't say anything for a long time. "I brought you back," I whisper.

She lets go of me and runs her fingers along the grooves of her name on the headstone. "I knew it. Somehow I knew. I'm ... not meant to be here. I was ... somewhere else." Her forehead wrinkles, like she's trying to remember where she's supposed to be. "The day on Brighton beach. That's where I was. I was with you on Brighton beach. Every day was that day."

Is she saying what I think she's saying? She *remembers* ...?

"Sam, I have to go back." A tear rolls down Eliza's cheek and falls off her chin. "I think it's where I'm supposed to be."

I don't want her to go. I love her so much, my heart is water-logged with it. We were supposed to grow up together. We were going to have such adventures. We were going to travel the world and call everywhere our home. We were going to turn our love into a family so that our love would travel down the years for ever and ever.

But those were only plans, and plans are no more substantial than dreams.

That future wasn't to be and I was an arrogant fool to challenge fate. I have made things so much worse. I look at my Eliza now. She's pale, thin and restless. She's almost hugging her gravestone and know it's all my fault. I imagine her on Brighton beach ...

She lurches forward onto her hands and knees, choking.

"Eliza?" I cry in horror. "What's wrong?"

She's retching hard, like she's coughing something up. Her mouth hangs open and her eyes stream. She puts a hand to her lips. A chunky lump passes up her throat and she coughs it into the palm of her hand.

It's the shell I stuffed in her dead mouth. "Oh Jesus ..."

"Sam?" she says. "What *is* that?"

I take it from her. "It's how I brought you back."

I think I know what I am to do. I have to destroy what I made, undo what I did. It's already unravelling. I can only pray that if I put things back the way they should be, the thing haunting my mother, that *leech* sucking out her life, will return with Eliza.

I wrap my fingers around the shell, ready to crush it in my hand.

"Ahem!" The dainty sound cuts into the silence of the graveyard. I turn and see the Milk Man leaning against a sloping Celtic cross. He's wrapped in a hooded charcoal-grey cape. The breeze drifts through his white hair. "Are you sure you want to do that, Samuel?" he asks.

"Who the hell is *he*?" Eliza asks.

"He played me," I say. "You played me!"

The Milk Man smiles. "Poor, sweet child," he says. "I merely helped you to realise your dark desires. Were you forced? Were you made to do anything against your will? Every diabolical deed was yours to own. This wickedness is yours and yours alone. You, dear boy, made a choice."

He's right, of course. I did make a choice. But it's never too late. It's never too late to be sorry. It's never too late to make amends. That's something Father and Aunt Marie would agree on.

"You're right," I say. "But I can make it better. That's what it's all about. It isn't about never doing anything wrong, but how you make it right."

"No returns!" The Milk Man's smile turns into a snarl. "Fool! What makes you think you get to start again? After every awful thing you've done – and you've done some unspeakable things – what makes you think you can ever be redeemed?"

I shake my head. "Because otherwise what's the point of anything?"

Eliza leans against me. Her body weighs almost nothing. "Samuel, please let me go ..."

"What makes you think the alternative will be any better?" the Milk Man says, his pink eyes ablaze.

"Returning Eliza to the grave won't heal your mother! It won't undo what you did!"

I close my eyes. Perhaps for the first time in my life I feel it. It's like an amber glow in the back of my head and in my heart. *Faith.* Not faith in what Dad believes, and not in what Aunt Marie believes, but faith in *good.* I have faith that good things can – and will – happen.

"Eliza, I love you," I say. "And I will love you, always."

Eliza strokes my face. "We're always together. Every day ... on Brighton beach. Remember that day, any time you miss me, and I'll be there."

"I will."

I kiss her and she rests in my arms. She's ready. She closes her eyes and a gentle smile crosses her lips. Oh so carefully, I lay her flat over her grave. She folds her hands in her lap.

"Goodbye, Eliza," I breathe in her ear.

I fix the Milk Man with a stare. I want him to see

this. I want to see him lose. I grip the shell as tight as I can. Its edges dig so deep into my palm it hurts. I squeeze and squeeze and squeeze. It cracks. Thick, black oil seeps out of my clenched fingers.

The Milk Man's body sags. His eyes roll.

My head pounds with my heartbeat and a shrill noise peals in my ears. The high pitch of it is unbearable.

I collapse next to Eliza.

She is the last thing I see before I screw my eyes shut.

Her face is serene.

Spring

I pull open the curtains and let light boom into my
bedroom. It's a bright Sunday and the apple tree
is thick with pink blossom. I'm meeting Fish at his
house to do some revision at eleven, but I really want
to visit Eliza first.

I dress in jeans and a checked shirt and hurry
downstairs. Mum is in the kitchen. She's stood in
the middle of the floor, hands on hips, looking lost.
"Herbal teas?" she asks.

"Middle cupboard," I say.

As I pass I give her a kiss on the cheek. She's
back at work now, but only part-time. She gets
tired easily and she's prone to forgetfulness, but the

doctors seem to think she'll make a full recovery. They *think* it was encephalitis – swelling of the brain. They aren't sure what caused it.

What I am sure of is that since the night in the graveyard, Mum's been a little bit better every day. I haven't seen the *thing* again. I think I closed the door that I so carelessly left open. If I made a cut in reality, it seems to be healing.

"Where are you going?" she asks.

"Just to see Eliza," I say.

"Lovely. If you see your father, tell him lunch is at two and we're not saving him a Yorkshire pudding if he's late."

"Will do."

It's warm enough to go out without a coat. I take my bike and ride at a gentle pace round the corner to the church. When I arrive, the bells are ringing out for the start of Sunday Service. I wave at Dad, standing proudly on the front steps welcoming his flock. Aunt Marie stands beside him, here for a weekend visit. They both wave back at me. "Where's your helmet, Sam?" Father shouts at me.

"Sorry!" I shout back.

Dad does not approve of Marie's lifestyle, and she disapproves of his disapproval, but at least the two of them are talking again. There's even talk of going to see their family in New Orleans in the autumn. I think that would be good for them and I've always fancied a holiday there too.

I ride on past the church and into the neat and tidy graveyard. I hop off and push my bike in and out of the headstones until I come to Eliza's. I swing my backpack off and take out a bunch of lilacs. They have mostly survived the ride over. I rest them on her grave next to the many other flowers.

I lie flat on my back, hands behind my head, and close my eyes. The kind sun beams on my face. It doesn't feel morbid to rest like this above Eliza's body, because I know she isn't here.

I take a deep breath and I *swear* I can smell

the salty pebbles, the sea and the candyfloss. I can hear the waves lapping and the joyful cries from the rollercoaster on the pier. I can hear her laughing.

Eliza and I on Brighton beach, together.

Are you a book eater or a book avoider – or something in between?

This book is designed to help more people love reading. It's a gorgeously Gothic tale of love, obsession and dark magic by a brilliant writer with stunning illustrations and a beautifully spooky cover to die for! *Grave Matter* offers so much for book lovers to treasure. And, at the same time, it has clever design features to support more readers.

You may notice the book is printed on heavy paper in two colours – black for the text and a pale yellow Pantone® for the page background. This reduces the contrast between text and paper and hides the 'ghost' of the words printed on the other side of the page. For readers who perceive blur or movement as they read, this may help keep the text still and clear. The book also uses a unique typeface that is dyslexia-friendly.

If you're a book lover, and you want to help spread the love, try recommending *Grave Matter* to someone you know who doesn't like books. You never know – maybe a super-readable book is all they need to spark a lifelong love of reading.